Ed and the Shirtmakers

by Andy Seed
& Rachael Smith

MAY 2018

D1580799

Bromley Libraries

30128 80241 204 2

Titles in Once Upon *Another* Time...

PRINCESS FROG-SNOGGER
BY TOMMY DONBAVAND & MARK PENMAN

LITTLE RED
BY BARRY HUTCHISON & MARK PEARCE

THE LEAGUE OF ENCHANTED HEROES
BY TIM COLLINS & JAMES LAWRENCE

THE BOY WHO CRIED ALIENS!
BY DANNY PEARSON & ABBY RYDER

GOLDIE LOCKED!
BY IAN MACDONALD & MARC ELLERBY

ED AND THE SHIRTMAKERS
BY ANDY SEED & RACHAEL SMITH

Badger Publishing Limited
Oldmedow Road,
Hardwick Industrial Estate,
King's Lynn PE30 4JJ

Telephone: **01438 791037**
www.badgerlearning.co.uk

2 4 6 8 10 9 7 5 3 1

Ed and the Shirtmakers
ISBN 978-1-78464-528-1

Text © Andy Seed 2016
Complete work © Badger Publishing Limited 2016

All rights reserved. No part of this publication may be reproduced,
stored in any form or by any means mechanical, electronic, recording
or otherwise without the prior permission of the publisher.

The right of Andy Seed to be identified as author of this work
has been asserted by him in accordance with the Copyright,
Designs and Patents Act 1988.

Publisher: Susan Ross
Senior Editor: Danny Pearson
Editorial Coordinator: Claire Morgan
Illustration: Rachael Smith
Designer: Fiona Grant

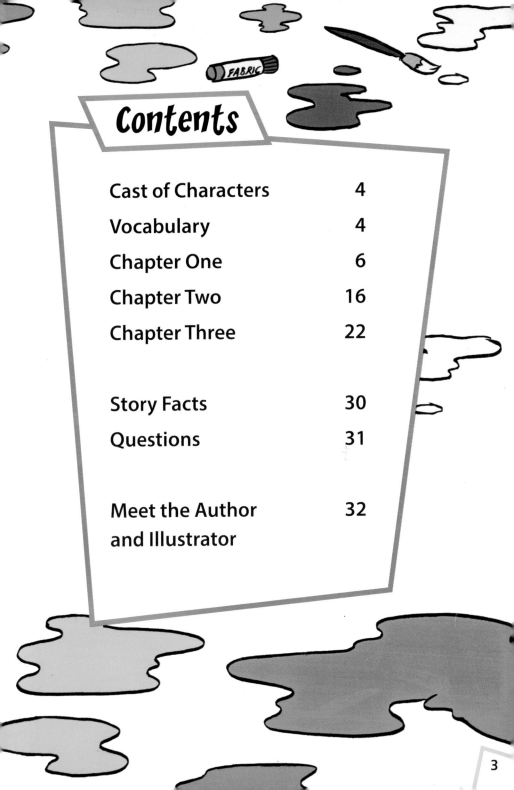

Contents

Characters

Ed

Maisha

Vocabulary

amazing	police
artists	popped
crashed	spaceship
moped	torches
nodded	youth club

Once Upon Another Time...

Chapter One
The Shed

"*AAAARRRGGGHHHH!*"

Ed was broke again. And fed up.

"I should have my own moped by now," Ed said to his friend Maisha. "Well, at least a new hat."

Maisha shook her head. "You're 14. What would you do with a moped?"

"That's not the point. I've sold loads of t-shirts to my mates – they all love them."

"The t-shirts you make are great," said Maisha. "They're funny."

"So why don't I have any dosh?" said Ed.

Maisha smiled. "Cos you always spend it on stuff to make more t-shirts, duh."

Maisha was right. Ed went, "Arrrggghhhh!"

Ed looked in his box of t-shirt stuff.

"One t-shirt left," he said. "I can't even think of a funny slogan to write on it."

Maisha said, "What about: I NEVER FINISH ANYTH..."

Ed smiled. "That's funny... but I never do finish anything."

"Sorry," said Maisha, "Oh, it's late – I'd better go now."

Ed put the t-shirt in the shed outside then went to bed. He didn't know that something outside was watching him.

The next morning Ed went to the shed. "I should try and finish that t-shirt," he said. "Then I could sell it."

At the shed Ed had a big shock. I mean BIG.

The t-shirt was not plain any more. There was a picture on it. A very funny picture of a baby's body.

Ed put the t-shirt on then looked in the mirror. He laughed so much he had to run to the loo.

Ed took the t-shirt to his youth club. Maisha was there.

"Did you do this?" he said.

"No," said Maisha. "But I wish I had – it's really funny."

A lad came up. "Cool t-shirt – I'll give you £10 for it."

A girl came over. "Wow, I'll buy it for £20."

Everyone wanted it!

A new kid came over. "I'll give you £40," he said.
The room went quiet.

Ed nodded. "Deal – I'm rich!"

With some of the money he made, Ed got two more plain t-shirts. He put them in the shed again.

He still didn't know who did the picture of the baby.

"It's a mystery and I love it," said Ed with a grin as big as a half-moon.

The next morning Ed's eyes nearly popped. Both t-shirts now had amazing pictures on them.

"Who could be doing this?" said Ed. "As crimes go it's a great one!"

Chapter Two
Artists

At the youth club Ed sold the t-shirts for £50.

Maisha said, "What is going on? It's potty!"

"I have a plan to find out," said Ed.

Ed told Maisha his plan.

"I'll buy three t-shirts and put them in the shed. Then I am going to stay up and sneak into the shed in the night."

"What if there's danger in there?" said Maisha.

"I'm going in with a frying pan," said Ed.

"Right…" said Maisha. "I'd better come with you."

Later that night they put the t-shirts in the shed and waited.

At 2am they burst in with torches.

There were two aliens in the shed painting the t-shirts!

ALIENS!

Ed and Maisha froze.

"Er, hello," said one alien. "Like our artwork?"

"Y-y-yes," said Ed.

"Don't worry," said the other alien. "We are artists on our planet. We don't eat kids. We were just bored."

Chapter Three
Cheese

The aliens told Ed and Maisha that their spaceship had crashed on Earth.

"To work it needs floop for fuel," they said.

"What's floop?" asked Maisha.

"I think you call it cheese."

"Oh, there's loads in the youth club kitchen," said Ed. "I'll get it for you." He ran off.

Ed ran to the youth club.

He opened a window and climbed in. But someone saw him.

As Ed came out, the police were there.

"I'm just getting cheese for some aliens," he said.

It didn't sound good.

They took him away.

The policeman told Ed to talk.

"Just tell me the truth, lad," he said.

"But the aliens really did draw pictures on my t-shirts."

The policeman laughed. Just then a big spaceship came past the window and the aliens waved to Ed.

The policeman fainted.

The police let Ed go and he went home. Maisha was there.

"I went to my house and got the aliens cheese," she said. "They fixed the spaceship right away."

"Cool," said Ed.

"They left this for you too," she said.

It was another t-shirt.

"I'm keeping this one," said Ed.

Story Facts

T-shirts got their name because they look like the letter T.

T-shirts first took off in the 1950s.

The first t-shirts were plain – logos were not used much until the 1960s.

There is about 8km of thread in one t-shirt.

About 2,000,000,000 (2 billion) t-shirts are sold each year.

The world record for the most t-shirts worn at once is 257.

The world's biggest t-shirt is 93m long and weighs 4500kg.

A t-shirt with a collar is called a polo shirt. It has nothing to do with mints.

Questions

What was Ed saving money up for? *(page 6)*

How old is Ed? *(page 6)*

How much did Ed sell the t-shirt with a baby on for? *(page 12)*

What time do Ed and Maisha burst into the shed with their torches? *(page 18)*

Who or what did they find in the shed? *(page 20)*

What t-shirt design would you come up with?

Meet the Author

Andy Seed loves cheese, football, Yorkshire, cats and cheese. He is the only author in the world to have really slipped on a banana skin (he thinks) and he is very glad to have the best job there is – writing books!

Meet the Illustrator

Rachael Smith is a comic creator and illustrator. She likes video games and cats. She has been drawing for most of her life. In fact, she'd be drawing right now if she wasn't typing this.